A Pod *of* Orcas

A Pod of Orcas

by Sheryl McFarlane

Illustrations by Kirsti Anne Wakelin

Fitzhenry & Whiteside

Text copyright © 2002 by Sheryl McFarlane c.9
Illustrations copyright © 2002 by Kirsti Wakelin.
Published in Canada by Fitzhenry & Whiteside,
195 Allstate Parkway, Markham, Ontario L3R 4T8

Published in the United States by Fitzhenry & Whiteside,
121 Harvard Avenue, Suite 2, Allston, Massachusetts 02134

www.fitzhenry.ca   godwit@fitzhenry.ca

10 9 8 7 6 5 4 3 2 1

National Library of Canada Cataloguing in Publication Data

McFarlane, Sheryl, 1954-
A Pod of Orcas : A Seaside Counting Book

ISBN 1-55041-681-2 (bound).--ISBN 1-55041-722-3 (pbk.)

1. Counting--Juvenile literature. I. Wakelin, Kirsti
II. Title.

QA113.M38 2002   j513.2'11   C2002-900927-8

U.S. Cataloging-in-Publication Data
(Library of Congress Standards)

McFarlane, Sheryl.
A Pod of Orcas / written by Sheryl McFarlane ; illustrated by Kirsti Wakelin. -- 1st ed.
[28] p. : col. ill. ;   cm.
Summary: There is so much to count at the seashore—one lighthouse, two freighters, three eagles… and on and on,
until you get to ten. Then a pod of orcas explodes out of the sea. At the end of the day, count from ten all the way
down again, as ten sailboats, nine fish boats, eight beach umbrella.
ISBN 1-55041-681-2
ISBN 1-55041-722-3 (pbk.)
1. Seashore. 2. Counting. I. Wakelin, Kirsti, ill. II. Title.
[E] 21 2002 AC   CIP

Fitzhenry & Whiteside acknowledges with thanks the Canada Council for the Arts, the Government of Canada
through the Book Publishing Industry Development Program (BPIDP), and the Ontario Arts Council for their
support of our publishing program

Design by Wycliffe Smith

For my three girls who kept me busy counting whales, eagles,

sailboats and seals, and for John whose love I could always count on.

— Sheryl

For my Grandma, my Mum and my Dad who brought books and art to me

and gave me the encouragement to make my own.

— K.W.

1

One lonely lighthouse
guides ships night and day.

2

Two giant freighters
drop anchor in the bay.

3

Three hungry eagles
soar upon the breeze.

4

Four treasure hunters
wade up to their knees.

5

Five fearless pirates

risk a leaky ride.

6

Six sturdy castles

battle with the tide.

7

Seven frisky faces
surface to explore.

8

Eight bright umbrellas
dot the sandy shore.

9

Nine salmon fish boats
set out for high seas.

10

Ten brilliant sail boats
fly along the breeze.

A super pod of orca

explodes the glassy sea.

10

Ten sleepy sail boats

shelter in the bay.

9

Nine salmon fish boats

head home for the day.

8

Eight bright umbrellas

drop and drift away.

7

Seven harbour seals

settle near the bay.

6

Six sturdy castles

melt into the sea.

5

Five fearless pirates

boast of victory.

4

Four treasure hunters
wish that they could fly.

3

Three stately eagles
scan the sunset sky.

2

Two loaded freighters

finish for the day.

1

One lonely lighthouse

guides them on their way.